Stony the road we trod,

Bitter the chast'ning rod,

Felt in the days when hope unborn had died;

Yet with a steady beat,

Have not our weary feet

Come to the place for which our fathers sighed?

We have come over a way that with tears has been watered,

We have come treading our path thro' the blood of the slaughtered,

Out from the gloomy past,

Till now we stand at last

Where the white gleam of our bright star is cast.

God of our weary years,

God of our silent tears,

Thou who hast brought us thus far on the way;

Thou who hast by Thy might,

Led us into the light,

Keep us forever in the path, we pray.

Lest our feet stray from the places, our God, where we met Thee,

Lest our hearts, drunk with the wine of the world, we forget Thee;

Shadowed beneath Thy hand,

May we forever stand,

True to our God, true to our native land.

Sing a Song

How *"Lift Every Voice and Sing"* Inspired Generations

By KELLY STARLING LYONS

Illustrated by KEITH MALLETT

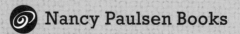 Nancy Paulsen Books

With love and gratitude for
James Weldon Johnson, J. Rosamond Johnson,
and the generations of children and adults
who passed their song on—K. S. L.

To Dianne—K. M.

Nancy Paulsen Books
an imprint of Penguin Random House LLC, New York

Text copyright © 2019 by Kelly Starling Lyons. Illustrations copyright © 2019 by Keith Mallett.
Nancy Paulsen Books is a registered trademark of Penguin Random House LLC.

Visit us online at penguinrandomhouse.com

Library of Congress Cataloging-in-Publication Data is available upon request.

Manufactured in China by RR Donnelley Asia Printing Solutions Ltd.
ISBN 9780525516095
1 3 5 7 9 10 8 6 4 2

Design by Marikka Tamura.
Text set in Rockwell Std.
The illustrations were drawn freehand and painted digitally.

Before you were born, a girl learned a song.

Her principal, James Weldon Johnson, and his brother, John Rosamond Johnson, had written the hymn for a celebration of President Abraham Lincoln's birthday.

The girl wanted to make them proud.

She hummed the song on her way home from school.

She practiced it as she did her chores.

On the big day—February 12, 1900—
she was part of a choir 500 strong.
Back straight, head high, heart and
mouth open, she sang.

Lift ev'ry voice and sing,
Till earth and heaven ring,
Ring with the harmonies of Liberty;

And she kept on singing as she grew up.
She taught it to her students when she became a teacher.
She crooned it to her husband as they journeyed
from Jacksonville, Florida, to a new life
in Pittsburgh, Pennsylvania.

She sang it when she rocked
her baby boy to sleep.
It was a part of her
she wanted to pass on.

And you know what?

Her little boy learned that song.

He listened to her hum it as she dreamed of
being able to teach again in her new home.

He heard his daddy sing it when the days
at the steel mill wore him down.

Then one day he stood in the choir loft and gazed
at the glowing faces. Back straight, head high,
heart and mouth open, he sang.

Let our rejoicing rise,
High as the list'ning skies,
Let it resound loud as the rolling sea.

And he kept on singing.
He sang it when he came back from
World War II and faced discrimination.
He sang it when he joined the NAACP.

He sang it with his wife
and to his baby daughter
as he rocked her to sleep.
It was a part of him
he wanted to pass on.

And you know what?
His little girl learned
that song. She sang it
each morning at school.

Then came the day that broke the nation's heart.

Dr. Martin Luther King, Jr., was killed.

The next morning, she saw her teacher cry.

Sobs replaced singing. Then whimpers and silence.

Who would lead them now?

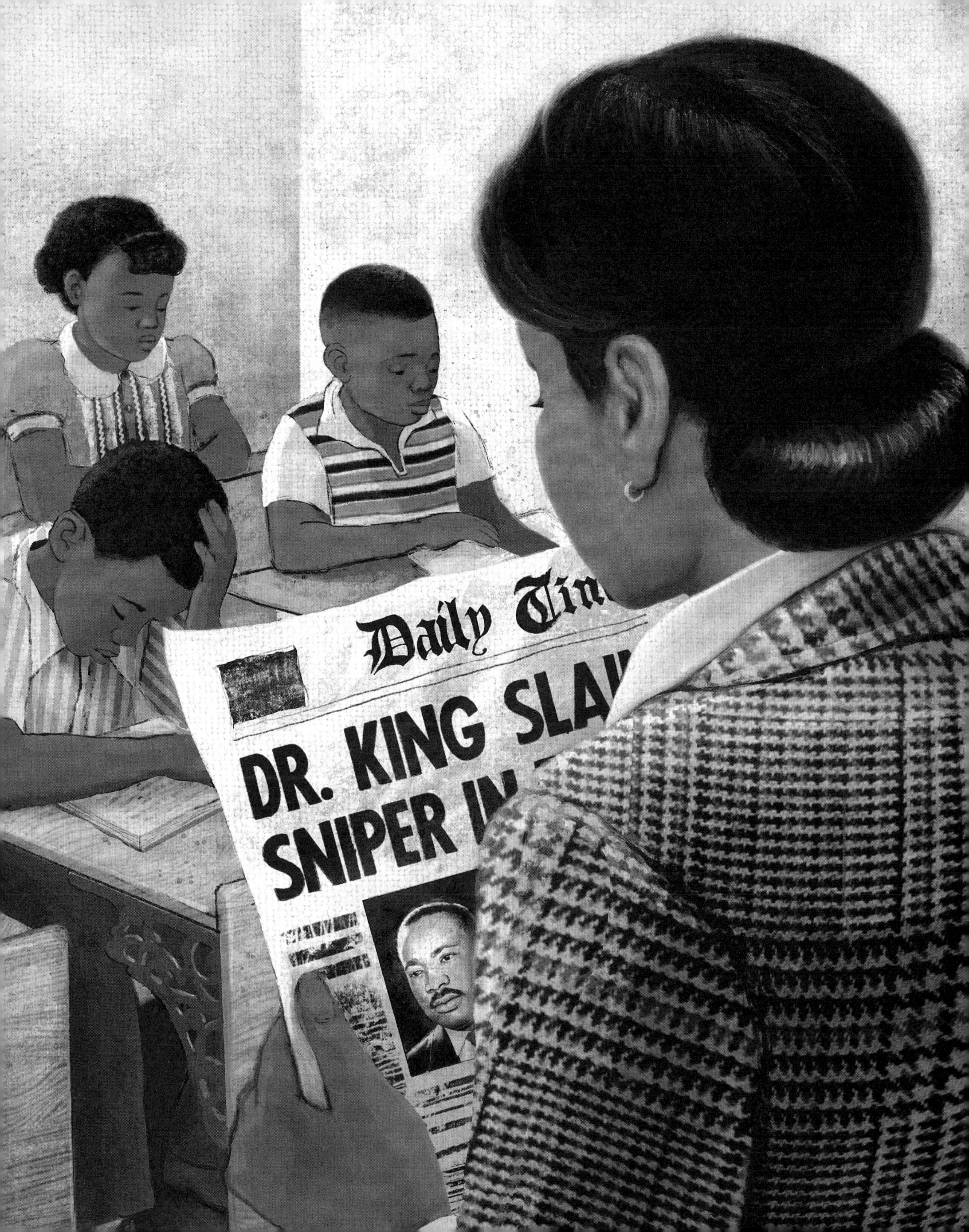

The headline reads "Daily Times — DR. KING SLAIN / SNIPER IN..."

The song whispered an answer.
Back straight, head high,
heart and mouth open, she sang.

Sing a song full of the faith that
the dark past has taught us,

And she kept on singing. She sang it at protests for equal rights and when she and her friends were jailed. She sang that song in her heart each time she won or lost a case as a lawyer.

EQUAL RIGHTS

STO
RAC

JUSTICE FOR ALL

JOB
R A
OW

I HAVE A DREAM

WE PROTEST INJUSTICE

END RACISM

WE SHALL OVERCOME

VOTI
RIGI
NO

She sang it to her baby boy
as she rocked him to sleep.
It was a part of her she
wanted to pass on.

And you know what? Her little boy learned that song.
Every family reunion opened with that anthem.
He sang because he had to at first. But then, something
changed. He saw the awe in his grandparents' faces,
saw the pride in his momma's and pop's. Back straight,
head high, heart and mouth open, he sang.

Sing a song full of the hope that
the present has brought us;

And he kept on singing. He sang it at his college graduation and when he opened his first business. He sang it at rallies to stand up against racism. He sang it holding his wife's hand at Black history programs and when he rocked his daughter to sleep. It was a part of him he wanted to pass on.

And you know what? His little girl learned that song.
And on another big day—September 24, 2016—
she stood in a crowd of thousands along with
her momma and daddy.

President Obama, the First Lady, and generations of one family rang the freedom bell. A dream born a century ago—to honor Black lives and contributions—had finally come true. The National Museum of African American History and Culture was officially open.

With the Washington Monument piercing the sky,
that little girl stared at the bronze building majestic
as a crown. As bells around the nation tolled in triumph,
she heard a voice rising too. Clear and strong, it was
a song she heard her parents sing. Back straight,
head high, heart and mouth open, she sang.

Facing the rising sun of our new day begun,
Let us march on till victory is won.

And you know what? That song is part of you.

Sing when you score a victory.

Sing when tough times get you down.

Sing and think of all the people who sang before you,

who carried on and pushed forward even

when everything was against them.

Sing and remember they never stopped believing.

Keep singing,

keep pushing,

keep passing it on.

Keep on keeping on.

Author's Note

I first heard "Lift Every Voice and Sing" in church as a little girl. I didn't understand all of the words, but I saw so much passion in people's faces and heard such pride in their voices as they sang that I could feel the meaning. This was a song that spoke to who we were. It was filled with reverence for all that Black people had overcome and achieved, filled with faith that we would keep pressing on and accomplish so much more. It connected us to our roots and reminded us of the strength we hold inside.

I sang this Black National Anthem many times over the years. I knew it was written by brothers James Weldon Johnson and J. Rosamond Johnson, but I didn't know the incredible journey of the song until I visited the Ritz Theatre and Museum in Jacksonville, Florida, my husband's and the Johnson brothers' hometown. There, I got a window into an amazing story I had to share. James Weldon Johnson was principal of the segregated, all-Black Stanton School. He and his brother wrote the song for a celebration of President Abraham Lincoln's birthday. James composed the lyrics. His students sang it in a chorus of five hundred voices.

Though the Johnson brothers moved away from Jacksonville and authored many songs, "Lift Every Voice and Sing" took on a life of its own. The children of Jacksonville taught the song to their children and students, sang it in their churches, and passed it on when they moved to new cities. Within a couple of decades, "Lift Every Voice and Sing" was spreading south to north and became the official song of the National Association for the Advancement of Colored People (NAACP). It was sung during the Civil Rights Movement; at family reunions, college graduations, and sporting events; played on radio stations and in houses of worship and homes. It became a popular hit when a version by singer Melba Moore landed on the *Billboard* charts, and made the news when Beyoncé sang it at Coachella.

The moments in this book were inspired by the song's journey and my family heritage. Like millions of others, my maternal grandmother's parents were part of the Great Migration. They moved from Alabama to Pittsburgh and sang "Lift Every Voice and Sing" in their new home. My mom and aunt were taught the song by their parents, and vividly remember being told in class about the day Dr. King was killed. The scene at the end was inspired by my going to the opening of the National Museum of African American History and Culture with my husband, kids, and family friends.

Today, "Lift Every Voice and Sing" is a symbol of faith, brilliance, resistance, and resilience. We survived slavery. We survived segregation. We'll overcome today's challenges and continue to soar. Young people can stand tall and draw strength from the song just like those in past generations. That's the message I want kids to hold in their hearts.

—Kelly Starling Lyons

Lift Every Voice and Sing

Lyrics by JAMES WELDON JOHNSON

Music by J. ROSAMOND JOHNSON

Lift ev'ry voice and sing,

Till earth and heaven ring,

Ring with the harmonies of Liberty;

Let our rejoicing rise,

High as the list'ning skies,

Let it resound loud as the rolling sea.

Sing a song full of the faith that the dark past has taught us,

Sing a song full of the hope that the present has brought us;

Facing the rising sun

Of our new day begun,

Let us march on till victory is won.